DANI and the Day the Bully CHANGED EVERYTHING

To Lorelei Anna —
Always be kind!
Best,
Donna DiMaio Rooney

DONNA DIMAIO ROONEY
ILLUSTRATED BY SALLY TAYLOR

SHEEPY
PRESS

Author Photo by Dorota Long. Illustrated by Sally Taylor

Sheepy Press

Softback ISBN: 978-0-578-17906-3
Hardback ISBN: 978-0-578-17907-0

Library of Congress Control Number: 2016909320

PRINTED IN THE UNITED STATES OF AMERICA

This book is dedicated to all the children.
You truly have the power to change the world.

Acknowledgments

A special thank you to the following people who have been instrumental to my book. My husband Jim; your continuous love and support in all that I do goes beyond measure. Your insight from the perspective of an educator has been invaluable. Ryan, your enthusiasm and belief that Mommy will get her book published kept me going. Together, I'm glad we named one of the main characters after your beloved stuffed animal Sheepy #1. My parents Evelyn and Alfred DiMaio — Mom, your constant prayers, faith, and encouragement are beautiful gifts that I cherish. Dad, although we miss you immensely, your words of wisdom continue to be heard to this day. Debbie Koke, my sister, for doing some final touch-up edits, especially the ones I missed. Godmother Celeste Sama, for believing in me. Andee Reda, my treasured friend, your farm animal knowledge was most helpful in making the characters authentic.

Thank you to the children who heard my book before it was published. Your positive feedback conveyed through drawings and letters, which hang above my computer, has been truly inspiring.

I am grateful to all of the above mentioned, plus my family, friends and those I've met along the way. Thank you for touching my heart. May kindness and love shine on you!

- D.D.R.

Chapter One

It was a warm spring afternoon and all was right with the world for eleven-year-old Dani, as she leaped off the school bus into the bright sunshine. "See you tomorrow, Mrs. Carpenter," Dani enthusiastically shouted, as she waved goodbye to her driver. Before the bus could pass the white post mailbox, Dani had skipped halfway down the hill to the rustic yellow farmhouse that had been in her family for five generations. "Mom, I'm home!" Dani hollered as she threw open the front door and tossed her green backpack on the floor.

After a warm motherly welcome, Dani scarfed down her snack at the kitchen table while conversing with her mom about the day's happenings. In a flash, she was outside soaking in the fresh air and smelling the fragrant spring flowers that had just bloomed. "Hum," Dani humorously said, "April showers really do bring May flowers," and laughed that she remembered the old familiar saying her dad repeated annually. Dani's glowing smile matched her sunny disposition as she blazed through each and every day. Just like her dad, Dani's curious brown eyes reflected the interest she had in the world around her medium-sized frame. As Dani explored about, her sandy blond ponytail swung to the beat of every lively step she took. Whether digging for worms or climbing trees, Dani did everything with much grit and vigor, just like her grandma who lived with them on the farm. It was evident that Dani was a farm girl through and through, right down to her faded denim overalls that had permanent traces of dirt woven into the fabric. At an early age her parents decided to call her Dani, instead of by her formal name, Danielle—the nickname suited her well.

Maintaining a farm took a lot of hard work, and Dani was happy she was old enough now to take on more responsibility, especially when it came to caring for the animals. The farm animals were her special friends, each with their own unique personality traits, which Dani loved. She deeply understood them, and in return they seemed to understand her perfectly. The family farm had a rhythm all its own, which Dani's heart seemed to beat right along to. Each animal's distinct sound filled the country air, as did the motorized clatter of the tractor, which Dani's father drove. Every afternoon, just like today, Dani made her rounds feeding the animals.

As she scattered feed for the chickens, Dani asked cheerfully, "What news do you have to report today?" Even though she had fed the chickens countless times before, she still marveled at the way they nervously ran circles around her, as though they were being chased by a playful puppy. Their *bac-bac* gossip sounds, Dani was certain, could be heard miles away. "I wouldn't change one note of your chatter, even if you all are talking to me at the same time," Dani announced as she headed to the chicken coop to collect their eggs. Tornado, whom Dani named from the moment she was hatched, always had a tender spot in her heart, and the feeling was mutual. Of all the chickens, Dani sensed Tornado had the most logic and seemed to lead the peeps out of sticky situations, like the time one of them got a foot tangled in the chicken wire. It was Tornado with her fast thinking, just like her talking, that pecked the wire until it loosened and freed the chick.

Another attribute of Tornado's that set her

apart from the other chickens in the coop was that she laid beautiful blue eggs. Tornado is known as an Easter Egger, which is a chicken that possesses the "blue egg" gene. People would always admire the unique color, which was striking next to the ordinary white and brown eggs. Those unfamiliar to the farm would inquire if the eggs had been dyed, to which Dani would proudly respond, "No, these are all-natural blue grade-A eggs!" At Easter time, Dani's family would invite all the children from the town to a giant Easter egg hunt. The secret ingredient to the egg hunt's success was that mixed among the colorful dyed eggs would be one of Tornado's. There was always a special prize given out to the child who found the genuine blue egg.

Next, it was off to Truffles and the piggies, which always sounded like a rock group to Dani! The pigs were the most joyful of all the animals on the farm – full of pure fun and delight, and boy were they hogs when they ate! They enjoyed splashing in the cool mud, which was most refreshing, especially during the sweltering summer days. Dani knew exactly how the damp mud squishing between her toes and layered thickly on her skin felt, ever since that sizzling August afternoon. It was on that day, two years ago, that Dani stood in the middle of the pen melting faster than an ice-cream cone. At that moment, the dark gooey mud reminded her of when ice-cream is dipped into warm chocolate and magically freezes into a hard shell. Without thinking twice, Dani kicked off her socks and shoes and with a running start slid into the muddy pen, where she plowed smack into Truffles' snout. That hilarious encounter generated Truffles' high-pitched squeal and Dani's infectious laugh that bonded the two forever as best friends.

The remainder of that day was spent playing until neither was sure who was covered with more mud. Ever since that time, Dani made it her tradition that a pig mud bath would be honored on the hottest summer day! As Dani replenished their food in the trough, she thought about what her dad mentioned the day before, how pigs are greatly misunderstood. She then recalled how they are super intelligent and don't even sweat a drop. As she giggled at the pig's comical snorting sounds and playfulness, she realized how easy it is to forget what her dad continues to teach her about these amazing animals. It was those gregarious traits she admired most about her beloved pigs, and in many ways they reminded Dani of her carefree self.

Directly across from the pen were the stables, where Lightning the horse was waiting for his weekly scrubbing and grooming. While taking a gander back at the pigs, Dani chuckled that she was going to bathe Lightning, when it was the piggies who were genuinely filthy! As Dani shampooed Lightning's long ebony mane and muscular legs, she recalled how the stallion won its first blue ribbon last year. Dani's family was proud that Lightning had won the race, and now knew his name matched his amazing speed. "Wow, you are handsome and fast, Lightning, and I suspect you know it too," Dani sang in a lyrical voice. Lightning thrived on success and it was evident the other animals looked up to him with great admiration and respect. Three times a week, Dani would jump on Lightning's back and gallop through the fields down to the stream. It was during those afternoon jaunts that Dani's spirit felt most alive and full of adventure. She secretly would pretend to be as magnificent and confident as Lightning.

Lightning's neighbor was Bell, the cow, who waited patiently for Dani's attention. "Okay, Bell,

I'm moving, so let's get shaking," Dani said as she plopped onto the worn wooden stool. As the warm milk squirted into the metal pail, Dani made up a breezy melody to accompany the rhythmic milking sound. As the pail filled up, Dani said with great compassion, "How are you feeling today, Bell?" Dani instinctively knew when Bell was tired or not feeling up-to-par, for she would move ever so slowly. Bell was born with one leg shorter than the rest, and at times her health was in fragile condition. She was born early on a beautiful summer morning at the exact time the Sunday church bells rang filling the clear blue sky with blissful harmony. At that moment, Dani's mother suggested they name the new calf Bell. Sweet Bell's inner beauty and great wisdom resonated with all the animals on the farm. After a while, the animals didn't take much notice of Bell's limp, since her calm and caring ways overshadowed her disability and paved the way. By taking care of Bell, Dani learned to have compassion for everyone – humans included.

After Dani hauled the heavy milk pails to the dairy, she made her way to the pasture by kicking a small stone up the steep gravel incline. The rolling hills of the pasture were dotted with whitish-gray sheep grazing on the tall, green grass. This picturesque scene was home to Sheepy #1 and the flock. As Dani lifted the rusty latch to the pasture, she ever so gently whispered, "Howdy," so not to startle them. Dani learned everything she knew about raising sheep from Grandma. "Oh, sheep are shy and stick together," Grandma often said.

As Dani bent down to fill the water trough she spotted a bright orange fox, like a flame, blazing in the distance. Instantly, an alarm went off in her head, as she could "hear" Grandma's voice saying, "Sheep are extremely vulnerable animals and you have to protect them, Dani." It was a familiar saying that Grandma had instilled in Dani ever since she was a little girl. Dani knew that when sheep face danger their natural instinct is to flee, not fight. Then, like clockwork, they herd together for safety. Within seconds, the fox had scurried away.

"I'll always protect you Sheepy #1 and the flock, so never fear Dani is here!" With a loving embrace, Dani wrapped her strong arms around Sheepy #1, and rested her head into her thick, wooly coat. In response to the hug, Sheepy #1 made her adorable baa baa sounds that indicated her genuine love for Dani. Sheepy #1 had always been a great source of comfort to Dani for as long as she could remember. Their unique roles as protector and consoler deeply intertwined their hearts.

During that tender moment, Dani thought how much Grandma loved Lamby #1, when she was a young girl, and could recite what had become her favorite story word-for-word. Pretending to be Grandma, Dani looked at Sheepy #1 and the flock, as though they were her attentive audience, and in her best impersonation spryly said, "I was your age, Dani, when the first lamb on the farm was born. She entered the world on the first day of spring, which was also the town's bicentennial. It was so exciting that the news made the local town paper, and snapped a picture of me holding my beloved Lamby!"

Not only did Dani know the story by heart, but the tale was best illustrated by the framed, now yellowed newspaper clipping, which hung above the living room fireplace mantel. Dani went on to say, "A countless number of lambs have been born on the farm since that historic day, but no lamb had received such fanfare until the birth of you, Sheepy #1!" It was three years ago, exactly a half century, on the first day of spring that Sheepy #1 entered the world. Now hanging next to Grandma's framed newspaper clipping, was another framed article. This one had a picture of Dani, grinning from ear-to-ear holding Sheepy #1 with a caption that read: *"I saw it most fitting to name her Sheepy #1 in honor of her great, great, great…gee, I lost track of the greats… grandmother. Lamby #1 of course!"*

"Wow, life really does come full circle," Dani said, as she gave the sheep a wink while strolling to the gate. As she lifted up the latch she said in a soft voice, "See you all tomorrow." Looking now from outside the fenced-in pasture, Dani added, "And don't forget, you can always count sheep if you can't fall asleep," which made her giggle.

After easily finding another stone to kick, this time down the steep hill, Dani fondly thought how she and Sheepy #1 shared an unspoken connection with Grandma and the late Lamby #1. As the sun was setting, like a giant orange beach ball fading behind the horizon, Dani held on to the thought of how the coincidental timing of the births bridged the generation gap that was steeped in a strong agricultural family heritage. She carried this thought with her, as she walked down the hill to the farmhouse. It had been another beautiful day, and it would all happen again tomorrow, or so Dani thought.

Chapter Two

The next afternoon, as the school bus made a halt at the faded white post mailbox, the driver called out, "Dani, Dani—we are at your stop!" Dani had been staring out the window, her eyes fixed in a gaze, daydreaming about the disturbing event that took place at school that afternoon. In a startled voice, Dani said, "Oh, I'm sorry, Mrs. Carpenter," as she slowly walked down the stairs to the pavement. The bus was long gone before Dani was even halfway down the hill heading toward home. Her farmhouse shone in the distance like a towering lighthouse symbolizing light and hope in the midst of darkness.

Finally arriving at her safe haven, Dani dragged her feet into the foyer and placed her backpack neatly on the hook. In a voice not much louder than a whisper Dani said, "Mom, I'm not hungry. I'm going to take a nap under the peach tree before doing my chores." After her mom felt her forehead, which confirmed she did not have a fever, she was given permission to do just that.

Dani nestled herself under a shady peach tree, which was anchored between the family farmhouse and the magnificent magnolia that was this week's main attraction. *Ah, it's too bad magnolia trees only bloom their pretty pink and white petals for such a short time*, Dani thought as she soaked in the fragrant perfume, while carefully finding a place to rest her head against the tree. Along with the blooming petals, the blue sky and lively farm weren't enough to lift the dark, heavy mood that consumed Dani. As she gazed up at the fluffy, white cotton-like

clouds that morphed into familiar shapes and faces floating by, Dani couldn't stop her mind from playing the terrible scene that occurred on the school playground.

Overnight, it seemed as though the new boy at school turned into a giant bully, teasing and tormenting one of Dani's classmates during outdoor recess. Her classmate was a slender, smart, and athletic boy who held the school record for being the fastest track runner. He was a nice guy and considered one of the popular kids. Purposely, the bully tripped him, and then quickly snatched his lucky keychain that hung from his front pocket. The keychain had been given to him by his grandfather, and everyone knew he wore it during his races. While the bully tossed and dangled the keychain, he started saying mean and untrue things about the boy, and even about his grandfather. The boy's immediate reaction was to fight back, but he refrained due to the bully's immense size. After several minutes, which felt like hours, the boy couldn't take the harassment any longer and broke down in front of everyone. What upset Dani the most was that no one, including herself, told the bully to stop. At least someone, anyone, could have told the teacher on recess duty, but no one did. Why didn't anyone say or do something? That was the unanswered question that kept playing over in Dani's mind, like someone frantically calling out for their lost dog, but only hearing the sound of their own voice echoing back. As the white, whimsical clouds continued to drift overhead, Dani finally dozed off into a deep sleep.

Chapter Three

While in a peaceful slumber, Dani began to dream about the farm, and the new animal that would be visiting—a big bull. "Did you hear?" said Tornado the chicken in a rapid voice to Bell the cow.

"Hear what, Tornado?" Bell asked.

"That a bull will be arriving on the farm today! Yes, a bull, I tell you!" Without skipping a beat, Tornado continued, "He comes from the neighboring town, and he'll be staying with us for the entire summer."

Bell wasn't the least bit amused but kindly said, "Thanks for the information," as Tornado frantically continued on her way to the pen. Bell, like all the other animals on the farm, could always count on Tornado for news briefs and gossip of the day. As Tornado approached Truffles and the piggies, she relayed the same news.

"Wow!" said Truffles the pig. "That's exciting, since we haven't had any new animals here at the farm in a really long time. I never met a bull before! Gee, I sure hope he likes to play in the mud!"

Lightning the horse overheard their conversation and chimed in, "Oh, I knew a very friendly bull a long time ago, who was also from one of the neighboring farms. I recall he was loads of fun— I wonder if perhaps they are related?" Both Tornado and Truffles were now wondering too.

Faster than a crow flies, the news got to Sheepy #1 and the flock. "Oh, I don't like the sound of this one bit, said Sheepy #1."

"Why?" Tornado immediately asked.

"By nature we sheep are shy, and we get very

nervous about meeting new animals," Sheepy #1 exclaimed.

Tornado just bobbed her head and hollered, "Well, suit yourself," as she raced back to the coop.

That afternoon, the bull arrived on the farm, along with the intense summer heat. He was big! Actually, he was gigantic in size, and didn't look the least bit friendly. However, the animals long knew from the wise Bell, that you can never judge a book by its cover, which seemed to apply to animals, too. It was sweet Bell who happened to be the first to meet the bull, as he grazed on the dried-up yellow grass.

"Hi, my name is Bell!" she cheerfully said. "Welcome to our farm."

However, the bull only looked up for a moment with an annoyed look on his face. He gave her a smirk, then went right back to eating. *Hmm, now that was a strange encounter*, Bell thought as she stood staring out to the pasture. *Well, maybe he's just not having a good day.*

A short while later the bull strolled near the pig pen. Truffles spotted him first, and without delay shouted out as though bubbles were assigned to each word, "Hi, it's nice to finally meet you. Feel free to jump in the mud anytime! It's a great way to cool off!" However, his invitation went unanswered as the bull gave all the pigs a look of disgust that seemed to pop those invisible floating bubbles in mid-air. While mumbling unpleasant words under his breath, the bull continued his stroll. Truffles, with mud on his nose, didn't quite understand why the bull didn't respond, and was left feeling somewhat uneasy.

As the bull continued checking out the farm, he was forced to stop, so as not to step on Tornado, who was standing directly in his path. With a chipper "Hello," Tornado stretched her short neck,

as though she were reaching for the sky, and looked up at the enormous bull who was now staring down at her. In a rambling, nervous voice Tornado asked a litany of questions without taking a breath, "Oh, beautiful day, isn't it? What's your name? Oh, my name is Tornado. Where are you from?" Her questions hit him like a small yet mighty torpedo. With just one step, the bull could have flattened Tornado. Although the thought did cross his mind, he decided to continue on his way, leaving the chick behind in the trail of dust he created with his massive hooves. With one swoop of his head, he noticed Sheepy #1 and the flock out in the pasture. Of course, they were huddled together looking like a colossal-sized cotton ball, so the bull thought he would leave them alone.

In the distance, behind the sheep pasture, the bull's eye spotted a galloping horse in the field doing leaps and jumps over well-positioned fences. Of course, it was Lightning, the farm's beautiful, prize-winning stallion. As the bull inched his way closer, he was better able to see how Lightning made each leap effortlessly and with perfection. Each prance and leap made the bull's red blood boil with green poisonous jealousy. When Lightning was done with his practice, he started to lightly trot to where the bull had strategically positioned himself. As the distance between them narrowed, Lightning's mind wandered back to when he was a young colt, and had been friends with a charming young bull who was playful and witty. Time goes by and things often change, and Lightning had always wondered about his friend.

Eagerly waiting to meet the bull, Lightning made eye contact and said in a pleasant voice, "Hi, my name is Lightning, and I've heard a lot about you!"

"Oh, yeah, what have you heard?" grunted the bull.

It was not the response Lightning was anticipating. "Ahhh, that you come from the next town over."

Reluctantly, the bull responded in an arrogant tone, "Well, I move around a lot." What Lightning didn't know was that the bull had been transported several times from farm to farm, because he couldn't get along with the other animals. Lightning had been curious to know if he knew his long-ago pal, but decided not to ask the question after the unfriendly introduction.

As Lightning turned his gaze, he could tell the bull spotted the award-winning blue ribbon that hung over the entrance to the stable. Lightning explained, "My grandfather won that ribbon many years ago, and gave it to me once he retired from racing. The next day, I had a race and won my very first ribbon. So, that's why I consider Grandfather's ribbon my lucky ribbon!"

Sounding not the least bit amused, the bull said, "That ribbon isn't such a big deal, you know. I've won a ton of ribbons for bigger things than you can imagine and didn't need one ounce of luck."

As the bull walked away, Lightning stood there dumbfounded, not realizing he just had been told a lie.

Chapter Four

The next morning Tornado, Lightning, Truffles, Bell, and Sheepy #1 all chatted in the sheep pasture as the flock grazed their breakfast. "What do you think of the new bull on the farm?" Bell posed the question to the others.

Of course, Tornado was the first to chime quickly in with her opinion of her strange encounter. "He wasn't friendly and didn't answer any of my questions!"

Truffles said, "The bull looked rather hot when I met him, so I invited him to cool off in the mud. However, with a look of disgust on his face, he just shook his head."

"Well, mud isn't for everyone," said Sheepy #1, "but at least he could have thanked you."

"That's right," added Bell. "I always say, there's no excuse for rudeness."

Everyone shared their odd experience meeting the new bull. Everyone except the dynamic Lightning, who seemed unusually quiet. "What about you, Lightning? Did you meet the bull yesterday, too?" asked Tornado.

With a slight bit of hesitation, Lightning said, "Yes, I did."

"Well?" said the others in unison. "I, uh, got the sense he doesn't like me very much."

"What, not like you?" Tornado said in disbelief.

"How can that be?" said Bell. "You are nice to everyone and so well-respected."

"Don't forget smart and fun too!" Truffles playfully exclaimed.

"Plus, kind and easy to talk to!" Sheepy #1 added.

"Does he know you are an award-winning stallion?" Tornado said as though she were conducting an interview.

"Well, yes, he does. And, I think that's the problem," Lightning said coyly, then quickly galloped off for his morning run.

The afternoon air felt heavy, as though it were laden with thick pea soup. A puff of dry dust that layered the ground, followed the bull as he once again surveyed the land and checked things out. He first noticed a group of animals clustered by the pig pen, which was located across from the entrance of Lightning's stable. Although Lightning would have rather stayed in the cool shelter of his stable, he decided to walk out so as not to be impolite. As Lightning was about to say hi, the bull purposely tripped him, which made the stallion lose his footing and stumble a few feet. Lightning was taken aback, and before he could regain his balance, the bull took his sharp horn and tore Grandfather's blue ribbon that proudly hung above the stable. Within seconds, the sentimental ribbon that meant so much to Lightning now had a giant rip where it read *First Prize*. Beautiful, blue-hued threads that were once woven tightly together were now all frayed and dangled wildly on the bull's horn. The commotion caught the attention of Tornado, Sheepy #1, Bell, and Truffles, who were across the way congregating near the pen.

So taken aback by what they just witnessed, they stood like statues and stared. Terrible, mean things were now venting out of the bull's mouth, and directed at Lightning, who was taking the verbal hits. "You aren't a real cool and award-winning stallion. Lightning, you know what you are? You are a baby who needs his lucky ribbon— or should I say pacifier!" said the bull. His poison continued,

"Now your luck has run out and you'll never win another race again!"

Lightning's first reaction was to fight and knock him down, but the magnitude of the bull was intimidating, even to Lightning. The bull was like an erupting volcano. Each word he yelled out was like hot molten lava, filling the air with untrue statements about Lightning, and about his grandfather. It was a brutal, verbal attack that had never before happened on the farm. The strong, handsome, smart stallion felt just the opposite of all those qualities, at that moment. Although he tried, Lightning was unable to conceal the pain any longer. His heart felt ripped in half, just like his grandfather's sentimental prize ribbon, and began to cry. As Lightning's tears flowed, the bull's hollering laughter became even louder. Even as the bull started to slowly walk away, Lightning could still hear his grating laughter loudly in the distance, which shook his confidence and body with fear.

Lightning's friends were all in shock at what they had just witnessed. However, no one uttered a single word. Just then the gray stratus clouds, which couldn't contain the moisture any longer, let a few raindrops fall. Soon it was pouring buckets, and all the farm animals scampered quickly for safe cover. Secretly, Bell, Sheepy #1, Tornado, and Truffles were each scared they could easily become the bull's next target.

Chapter Five

The next morning dawned all too quickly for Lightning, Tornado, Bell, Sheepy #1, and Truffles, for none of them was anxious to wake up and greet the day. Each of them was still shaking from yesterday afternoon. However, farm life goes on, and before long they were each busy doing what they do best. Everyone but Lightning. In the safety of his stall, Lightning stayed there all morning, barely moving a muscle. His self-confident demeanor drastically changed to a somewhat shy and timid horse. The other animals seemed to be going on with their day, although didn't feel totally themselves either. Each one was plagued with the same recurring thought. If Lightning, the beautiful, award-winning stallion was publicly humiliated by the bull, then it could happen to them too.

Tornado decided to skip her gossipy, daily morning news briefs, since she wasn't quite in the mood to talk. Instead, she tried hard to conceal her blue eggs, which she knew would garner negative attention from the bull.

"He'll surely think my eggs are unusual and odd," Tornado mumbled to herself as she covered them with strands of hay, so not to be ridiculed.

Fear seemed to unwelcomingly embrace each of the animals who found themselves as bystanders at yesterday's bullying spectacle. In fact, even the wise and calm Bell had become a bundle of nerves. Years ago, she learned not to focus on her disability, but rather on her ability. She gracefully proved to herself, and to others, that her limp didn't define who she was as a cow. However, today she was thinking just the opposite. *Oh, if the bull notices that I have a limp, I'll surely be his next target. What will happen if he's walking behind me and I'm not moving fast enough? What will happen if he pushes me and I fall and can't get up?* What-ifs were badgering Bell's mind, as her heart seemed to race a mile a minute.

Over at the pasture, Sheepy #1 told the flock she was unhappy when she first learned that a bull would be spending the summer. Now, Sheepy #1's worst fear imaginable terrorized her entire being, and she felt like a wooly blanket of nerves. Even though she tried to count sheep, she couldn't sleep a wink last night. Needless to say, the flock herded together ever so tightly, and never left each other's side.

As the morning quickly faded to the height of noon, so did the rising temperatures, which soared well into the nineties. On any hot afternoon, it was a sure thing that Truffles and the piggies could be found cooling off in the squishy, gooey mud. But not this sizzling summer afternoon. No, this day felt entirely different. There was no way Truffles would be caught with mud on his nose, or anyplace for that matter, while the bull was on the premises. Acting out of character, Truffles kept impeccably clean on what became the hottest day on record.

When the day came to a close, Lightning, Tornado, Bell, Sheepy #1, and Truffles each seemed to have successfully avoided the bull. This extreme behavior of altering their personalities kept up for two painfully long days. The farm animals were not joyful, as they had been before the bull arrived. They each now lived in fear, and their only goal was to survive the day by going unnoticed.

Lightning had become quiet, depressed, and felt all alone. It wasn't just the fact that the bull humiliated him in front of his friends, but that his friends didn't come around anymore. He felt as though no one cared, and that left him extremely sad and lonely. What Lightning didn't realize was that the bullying he experienced also affected the animals who had been bystanders to the ugly event. The farm that had long symbolized a place of joy and safety now felt exactly the opposite.

Chapter Six

On the third morning, since the bullying, Tornado decided she needed to talk with the wise Bell about the anxiety and fear she was feeling. At first, she couldn't find Bell in her usual spot. However, after some searching, Tornado noticed her lying down in the tall, brown grass as though she were wearing a camouflage suit, so as not to stand out. To Tornado's surprise, Bell was feeling the exact same way.

"Then, what are we to do?" blurted Tornado.

"I've been contemplating that same question for days," Bell said in her soothing voice. "I remember my mother telling me, when I was a young calf, that no one can make you feel fear, unless you give them the power to do so."

"So, we've given the bull the power?" Tornado said as though a light bulb had switched on.

Bell motioned with a nod of her head, then said, "We need to have a meeting with all those who witnessed the bullying the other day. Would you quickly alert Truffles and Sheepy #1 that a meeting will be held in one hour at the sheep pasture?"

Without blinking an eye, Tornado fluttered on her way, doing what she enjoyed and did best – informing, updating, and spreading news.

Bell was the last one to arrive at the pasture. She was a bit out of breath, since it took much of her strength to walk up the steep hill. Bell's three strong legs compensated for her one weak leg, but still it was a struggle. Tornado greeted Bell at the entrance gate as though she were the keynote speaker of an event, and escorted her to where Truffles and Sheepy #1 and the flock were gathered.

"I'm glad we are all here together," blurted out Truffles. "I've missed everyone and the fun we used to share! I also miss me. Sadly, I'm no longer the happy pig I once was," shared Truffles.

"I'm different now, too," chimed Tornado. "I've been trying to alter who I am, just so I don't attract the attention of the bull."

"Everything now feels different, and I don't like it one bit," Sheepy #1 added to the conversation.

"Well, everything is different, but we don't have to be," stated Bell. With their eyes each fixed on the wise Bell, they hung on to each word she began to utter, as though she were giving them a formula to a complicated puzzle. And, in many ways, she was.

"What happened to Lightning is the most terrible thing we have all experienced here on the farm. The bull's cruel act not only humiliated

Lightning, but also left us feeling vulnerable and afraid. Fear has taken over each of us, because we don't want to become the bull's next victim. What makes each of us special and unique is exactly what we've been trying to hide from the bull."

Tornado quickly added, "You mean, the way I have been trying to conceal my blue eggs with hay?"

"And me staying impeccably clean?" Truffles squealed out.

"Yes, that's exactly what I mean," stated Bell. She then said, "I'm ashamed to admit it, but I've been doing the same thing—by trying to conceal my limp."

"We sheep do stick together when frightened, but it's not customary for us to spend 24 hours a day glued to each other's side," Sheepy #1 added to the remarks of her friends.

Bell continued, "However, beyond the fear, what I feel most guilty about is that I have not reached out to Lightning during this emotional and disturbing time."

"Me, too," said the others, as though they were part of a chorus.

Sheepy #1 blurted out, "I know how important it is to be reassured, yet I neglected to comfort Lightning."

"After all, he's our friend," said Truffles. "Why didn't one of us say something to the bull or help Lightning?" Just then, you could have heard a pin drop in the grass, as silence filled the air after Truffles posed the question. It was the same question the others had been thinking, but didn't have the courage to ask.

Bell finally broke the silence. "It is true that fear and fear alone has held each of us back from confronting the bull and comforting Lightning. No one can make you feel inferior, unless you give them the power to do so. We are all guilty of giving the bull that power. However, we need to change our thinking and our actions, in order to take back our loving farm, resume being ourselves, and end this terrible act of bullying."

Now all the animals were excitedly talking at the same time and asking, "How?" "How?" "How?"

"I'll tell you how," Bell calmly said. "First, we need to stick together. There is strength in numbers."

"I'm for that!" Sheepy #1 exclaimed.

Bell continued, "Next, we need to rally around Lightning and say we are here for him. Finally, we can't be bystanders any longer. From this day forward, we each need to stay alert to what is happening on the farm."

"I always do!" Tornado proudly shouted.

Lastly, Bell said, "We need to stand up to the bull—or to anyone, for that matter." The excited bunch seemed to quickly lose their sizzle when Bell made that last point.

"I'm never at a loss for words, but what would I say to the bull?" rattled Tornado.

"I don't even know how to be mean!" exclaimed Sheepy #1.

Bell quickly jumped in, "It's not about being mean. It's about telling the bull his behavior is wrong and we aren't going to tolerate it any longer on this farm. However, the tricky part is coming up with a creative way to get Lightning, or anyone that is being picked on by the bull, out of harm's way, without getting hurt ourselves."

"You mean diffuse the situation?" Truffles declared.

"Exactly!" said Bell. "Let's all meet at the chicken coop at sunset, and by then, I should have a plan in place. In the meantime, I hope you each get a chance to visit with Lightning, and invite him to tonight's meeting."

Chapter Seven

Like a bolt of energy, Tornado was the first to run out of the pasture and skidded into Lightning's stable. Of course, she wanted to be the first to voice her concern to Lightning, and invite him to the evening meeting. Sheepy #1 began to gently loosen her tight hold on the flock, knowing the others would stick by her, if needed. Truffles merrily strolled down the steep hill back to his pen, hoping things would go back to normal. Bell, on the other hand, took her sweet time as she gingerly made her way down the steep hill, being careful not to fall. She was consumed in thought, thinking how she would devise a plan that would not only empower the bystanders, but also every animal on the farm.

Before the magnificent orange sun, resembling a giant egg yolk, disappeared into the horizon, the foursome had once again gathered for the second time that day. Normally the coop smelled like a mixture of hay and eggs. However, this evening, it had the amazing aroma of homemade peach pie that filtered in on the warm summer breeze from the farmhouse next door. The last one to enter the coop was Lightning. After he received smiles and a warm and loving embrace from his friends, Bell started the meeting.

"First, Lightning—we are each sorry about what happened to you the other day. This meeting is about not letting that cruel act of bullying happen again to you, or to any other animal on this farm."

Before she could continue, Tornado jolted out, "I noticed the bull today, while I was talking with the peeps! I was scared he would come over to the coop, but luckily he just kept on walking."

Truffles jumped in, "That's because you were with the peeps."

Bell knew by the confused look on Tornado's face that she needed to further explain and said, "Deep down inside, a bully is a coward, so they usually target just one animal and not a group."

Sheepy #1 asked, "Why did the bull act the way he did to Lightning? Who would want to be so mean?"

"That's a good question," Bell said. "In fact, I gave that same question a lot of thought these past couple of days. Perhaps the bull must have a problem and took his anger and frustration out on Lightning. However, that does not give him an excuse for his behavior, nor does it give him a right to take out his anger on someone else."

For the first time, the group heard from

Lightning. "When I first met the bull, he seemed annoyed that I knew he had come from the neighboring farm. All I was trying to do was make friendly conversation."

Tornado's inquisitive mind was now going at high speed, like a detective wanting to figure out what the bull was hiding. Lightning continued, "The next day when I told the bull about Grandfather and my lucky ribbon, he became enraged."

Truffles quickly said, "It sounds to me he's a bit jealous of your success."

Sheepy #1 added, "And that you have a loving grandfather."

Bell said, "That could all be true. However, we can only speculate until we know for sure."

Lightning then revealed, "But what also hurt was that none of you stepped in to help or console me as I was being bullied. I felt all alone and terrified. It wasn't until Tornado stopped by this morning to invite me to tonight's meeting that made me feel that perhaps you all do care."

There was a long pause of silence followed by teardrops falling from the faces of those in attendance. Sheepy #1 was first to break the uncomfortable quiet. "I do care, and I'm so sorry I didn't comfort you during that vicious attack. I was scared and didn't know what to do."

Tornado jumped in, "I'm sorry, Lightning, that I didn't stop by earlier to see how you were doing."

After loudly blowing his nose, Truffles finally said, "You are my friend, Lightning, and I'm embarrassed that I didn't act like one to you. Can you forgive me?"

Bell also was teary-eyed and like the rest spoke from the heart. "I'm deeply sorry, too, Lightning. Fear prevented us from acting the way we should have. We all thought if the bull was able to mock you, the beautiful and strong stallion, what would he do to us, especially since our differences are obvious."

Lightning was touched that his friends truly did care and said, "Yes, I forgive you all."

After a group hug, Bell said, "I hope the plan I've outlined will change how we bystanders react in the future, should such an attack ever happen again."

When the animals heard the word *plan* they each leaned in closer to hear what the wise Bell was about to tell them.

"Standing up to the bull will perhaps be the most difficult thing I or you could ever imagine. In fact, finding the right words, especially during a high stress time, could jeopardize the situation and maybe even make it worse. Of course, we want to help the victim, but don't want to become one either. We will each carry a small sign attached to a ruler, approximately 12 inches long by 1 inch wide. If any of us notice Lightning or another animal on the farm getting harassed by the bull, we will take out our sign and hold it up high. The ruler-sized sign will act as an alert to others that something is terribly wrong. In bright, bold lettering the sign will read WE STAND WITH OUR FRIEND AND STAND UP TO BULLYING! STOP BULLYING NOW!

Bell further explained that the purpose of the sign would be twofold. First it would speak volumes to the victim that he or she was not alone. Secondly, it would send a strong message to the bull that his behavior would not be tolerated and needed to stop now!

Sheepy #1 then busted out with enthusiasm, "So we band together!"

"Yes," Bell said. "The more animals that stand up to the bull by holding their sign in the air, the more our actions will symbolize that he is now the one who stands alone."

"What happens if no one spots the bullying?" asked Tornado.

Bell reassuringly said, "I'm sure several of us will notice, since bullies like an audience. It makes them feel powerful."

Tornado concluded, "So, we were the audience the other day?"

"Yes," said Bell. "We were bystanders who sadly did nothing and let the abuse continue, while we watched. However, from this day forward that is all about to change."

All the animals started to feel empowered for the first time since the incident. Now it would be easy for them to show their support by waving a sign in the air with a powerful message to the bully. Best of all, they wouldn't have to utter a word in order to do the right thing. Sheepy #1 even felt fine about participating in this act of noble bravery. After all, if she didn't have to say a word, and others on the farm would stick close by her side, then she was fine with Bell's ingenuous plan.

"Now, we have no time to lose," stated Bell. So all through the night, Tornado, Sheepy #1, Truffles, plus Lightning and Bell worked hard to make fifty signs, enough for every animal on the farm to have one. They carefully cut the wood scraps in the coop to exactly ruler size. Tornado suggested that the signs be painted red. However, Lightning was fast to explain that horses, like himself, are color blind to red and green.

"Me too," added Bell. "All cattle, including bulls, are also color blind to those two colors, despite the myth that bulls charge at the color red."

"How very interesting," said Truffles. After a quick discussion about the color wheel spectrum, they settled on the color blue. Luckily for the friends, three buckets of sky-blue paint were found in the back corner of the coop. A few coats of paint easily transformed the plain wood into the making of a sign. Tornado dug out a couple of thick black markers she had stashed away, which were used to complete the job once the paint had dried.

Chapter Eight

As the sun rose expelling the darkness, the farm was gently woken by the dawn of a brand new day. Tornado and the peeps quickly delivered the signs to all the animals on the farm, along with Bell's precise instructions. By then, most of them had heard about the brutal bullying that had happened to Lightning, and they were frightened too. Magically, Bell's plan replaced the fear each of the animals had been feeling since the bullying attack with a new sense of purpose, camaraderie, and bravery. As the animals carried on with their day, they were now a combination of police and hero in the making— first, by keeping a watchful eye out for any bullying on the farm, and then by supporting the victim while standing up to the bully. Having the ruler-sized, blue sign strapped onto the side of their leg or back gave them each a new sense of security. It was really only a sign, but the sign symbolized power and a bright beacon of light that would alert the rest. No matter what type of animal they were, big or small, fast or slow, they could count on one another. It was something Sheepy #1 and the flock instinctively had done for years.

As the noon sun desperately tried to peek unsuccessfully out from behind the clouds, Tornado hummed a chipper tune as she skipped past the red barn. Her wings flapped freely now that she delivered the last sign. In the distance, she could see Lightning, Sheepy #1, and Truffles gathering, like they often did, outside the pig pen. Tornado was anxious to meet up with her friends and share the news that all fifty signs had successfully been delivered. As Tornado was just about to approach the pen, the bull appeared.

"Hey, you down there. I'm talking to you, little chicken," the bull hollered. Tornado immediately started shaking, and was sure she lost a feather or two. Just as the bull was about to mock Tornado's petite size, he spotted Bell slowly limping to the pen. His attention was now off of Tornado, and on to an even easier target – a cow with a bum leg. As the bull stared at Bell with his glaring gaze, he sharply said, "Just learning how to walk?"

Before Bell could answer, he purposely pushed her, so she would lose her balance and fall. With a loud thud, Bell fell to the ground. Her bad leg took the brunt of the fall, and now she was lying on the ground with her legs tangled and in tremendous pain. Tornado quickly took out her blue sign and standing on her tippy toes, held it high in the air as though she was reaching for the cloud-covered sky.

Lightning, Truffles, and Sheepy #1 all came running to the rescue, while unstrapping their sign to join forces with Tornado. Now the bull was surrounded by sky blue signs.

"What's this?" he said with a confused look on his face. Then he read the signs: WE STAND WITH OUR FRIEND AND STAND UP TO BULLYING! STOP BULLYING NOW! He looked down at Bell and said, "You are nothing, you lame cow!"

He waited for a response from the crowd. No one laughed or chuckled. No one even looked afraid of him. Instead, there was silence that seemed to speak louder than anything he had ever heard before. Soon, many of the other animals on the farm noticed the blue signs waving wildly in the air. They quickly ran to the scene, like firemen called to a fire, and one by one held high their blue signs, which made a striking contrast to the gray

sky above. Within what seemed like seconds, the bull was surrounded by animals that were not going to tolerate his behavior. Not with Lightning. Not with Bell. Not with anyone!

Bell was so deeply touched by the outreach of love and support from her friends that she found the strength within to get up from off the ground. Soon she was standing on all four legs, looking directly into the bull's eyes. Bell calmly and powerfully said, "It is true, I do have one leg that is weak and crippled, but I won't ever let that keep me down." Bell then quickly unfastened the sign from her side, and held it high while saying, "Together with my friends, I take a stand against bullying."

The bull, for the first time, was bewildered and said nothing. Now it was perfectly clear to him that he stood alone in his mean endeavor, and that this farm was not going to accept his behavior any longer. As the bull stared at what seemed like an ocean of blue signs surrounding him, he felt as though a tidal wave knocked him down. In fact, at that moment, the giant bull felt as small as an ant, wishing he could hide himself in the ground.

Lightning somehow found the courage to say, "What you did to me a few days ago hurt my feelings. Why were you so cruel? Why did you purposely damage my lucky ribbon that had sentimental value to me?"

With his head hung low, the bull said, "You reminded me of my past." He continued, "After being moved from farm to farm, I finally found happiness at the last place. My new friends, so I thought, looked up to me because I was fast. However, once the new stallion arrived everything changed. That horse was faster than me, and I became enraged with jealousy. I thought his amazing speed would get the attention of my friends, and I would be left alone once again. In my mind, being fast meant I would have friends. It wasn't until I had a fight with the horse, and sprained his ankle, that the farmer shipped me off to where I am now." All the animals looked at each other, as they tried to comprehend the story that had just been told to them.

Everyone thought the bull was done with his true confession. However, to their surprise, he was just getting started. It was as though the flood gates of the bull's heart were beginning to open. "When I saw you, Lightning, I got mad that you were fast, and that your grandfather loved you enough to give you his prized ribbon." Now the bull's eyes were filling up with tears and with great courage said something he never revealed before. "It's not just that I want to be fast, but that I want to be loved." Except for the slight summer breeze that blew the windmill in circles, the world for that moment seemed quiet and still. Even though Bell's leg was throbbing in pain, she could sense the bull's emotional pain was even worse.

Bell broke the hush and said, "Thank you for telling us the truth, for that must have taken a lot of courage. However, that is not an excuse to hate Lightning for being fast. Before you arrived on our farm, we were all well aware of our strengths and weaknesses. We looked at our differences as being unique. For example, even though I limp and walk slowly, that doesn't take away who I am inside. Tornado may be small, but she can talk quickly and relay information faster than the internet. Did you know Tornado even lays magnificent blue eggs?"

"Oh!" said the bull, not realizing that unusual fact.

Bell continued, "Sheepy #1 is shy by nature, but she is the best source of comfort you'd ever want. Truffles is usually covered with mud, but you'll never see him sweat, because pigs don't have sweat glands.

I could go on and on about each one of us here. You see, on this farm we celebrate our differences, which makes us special. It makes us who we are. Sadly, you mocked us in order to feel better about yourself."

Now the bull was beginning to understand. "Well," said the bull, "I guess I never thought about it that way before. But if I'm not fast, then I'm nothing! If only I had time to train instead of being moved from farm to farm and from country to country."

Tornado, now feeling more composed than earlier, inquisitively asked, "You lived in a foreign country?"

The bull really didn't want to tell them that he spoke more than one language, since it was something he always felt embarrassed about. Now with all the attention back on him, he blurted out, "If you really must know, I was born in Italy, and lived in Spain, France, and Switzerland before coming to America."

Truffles was now fascinated, as was the entire group, and said, "That means you must speak other languages, right?"

Feeling as though his entire history was being exposed, the bull annoyingly said, "Yes, I do. So what!"

The group once again was taken back by the bull's sharp tone. Bell said, "I get the sense you don't think that's cool, do you?"

With no way out of the question, the bull was forced to explain. "You see, when I came to America I had a difficult time learning the English language, since I already was fluent in Italian, Spanish, and French. Every farm I went to, I was made to feel different. All I wanted to do was fit in, so I worked hard to lose my accent and perfect my English."

Sheepy #1 said, "So, did you fit in then?"

No one was surprised when the bull answered, "No, I never did."

Bell said, as though speaking for the group, "Until now," and gave a big smile to the bull that seemed to radiate directly to his heart. Just then, the clouds overhead started to disperse, giving way to the blue sky that was there all along. Bell continued, "Your English is perfect, but don't abandon your talent for speaking other languages. That is a gift, and one many of us wish we had as well."

The bull was dumbfounded, for he never thought speaking another language was a gift, but if Bell said it was, then perhaps it was true. Sheepy #1 said, "We have three goats on the farm that speak French, and I sure wish we could communicate with them. Can you teach me to speak French?"

Tornado added, "That would surely help me too, so I won't have to mime my daily news briefs to the goats." Overcome with emotion, the bull was only able to nod his head with an eager yes!

For the first time, the bull genuinely felt loved and accepted. He sincerely said, "I hope you all can forgive me."

"There's only one small problem," Truffles said. The bull now wondered what that could be, as he waited with anticipation. "We don't know your name."

Everyone chuckled, including the bull. It was a much-welcomed relief from the tension-filled day. Even the sun seemed to be smiling as it finally broke through the thick gray clouds, changing the day's mood from gloomy to cheerful. "Toro," said the bull. "My name is Toro, which means bull in Italian!"

One by one, every animal in the crowd put down their sign. With a heartfelt welcome they all applauded the bull, and the start of a blossoming new friendship.

Chapter Nine

In the days and weeks that followed, everyone on the farm happily noticed a positive change in Toro, the bull. Instead of walking on eggshells, like the animals previously did, they felt once again comfortable in their own skin. The farm was back to being the safe and warm home it had once been, but with just a little twist. On any given day, Toro could be found in the coop, pasture, barn, pen, or dairy teaching the farm animals how to speak Italian, French, or Spanish. Instantly, the farm became a giant classroom for all.

One day, as Bell was being milked she heard Toro explain to the peeps, "Milk is leche in Spanish."

Hearing foreign words for ordinary things added a unique multi-cultural dynamic to the all-American farm. For the first time ever, Toro realized he did have a talent. Sharing his knowledge and teaching others made him feel good about himself. In fact, the more he helped, the more he wanted to give of his time and talent.

"Ah, you see, a little love and understanding can go a long way," exclaimed Bell to Tornado, Truffles, Sheepy #1, and Lightning as they lounged near the pen waiting for Toro to join them for their daily afternoon chat.

"And empathy, too," added Truffles.

The only concern the five of them had now was that summer was quickly coming to an end, which meant Toro would soon be on his way. As Toro approached the pen, he seemed to have an even bouncier step in his stride, which turned to skipping. "I'm staying! I'm staying on the farm!"

shouted Toro. His wide smile could not contain the overflowing love that poured from his heart. "The farmer said I don't have to leave. So I'm staying right here. Right here, where I belong."

Chapter Ten

"Dani! Dani! Dinner is ready, come inside," shouted Dani's mother from the front door of the yellow farmhouse. Eventually, the words penetrated through Dani's deep slumber, and woke her from the long afternoon nap she had been enjoying. "Dani, do you hear me? Dinner is ready."

"Coming, Mom," a yawning Dani said from her toasty napping area under the peach tree. The blue afternoon sky she fell asleep to had magically transformed to a tapestry of exquisite colors. As the sun started to set, Dani thought, *Gee, I wonder where Toro is?* Looking left then right she said out loud, "No, what am I thinking? We don't have a bull. I must have been dreaming!" As she sat motionless watching the sun slowly hide behind the horizon, Dani started to vividly remember every detail of her dream. Then, like a spark, she remembered the bullying incident that happened earlier that afternoon at school, and how that made her feel.

"Dani, are you okay? The farm animals ate; now you need to eat too," her mother yelled from the house.

"Yes, I'm fine, Mom. I'm sorry—I'll be right in," Dani said. As she slowly stood her waking body up, she thought of Bell getting herself up off the ground, in order to stand up to the bull. At that exact moment, her dream and reality joined forces in her mind. Instantly, Dani knew if there was to be an end to bullying at her school, it would need to start with her and the other bystanders. After all, they were the majority. She would also need to let the boy who was bullied know that he was not

alone. If Dani's farm animal friends could stand up to bullying, then she was determined to get her school to do the same.

Dani had always been a girl who would walk to the beat of her own drum, and she wasn't about to let fear change her tempo, not even slightly. Perhaps in time, Dani and her classmates could even befriend the bully. Anything felt possible now, since waking from her dream. Running to the front door, and feeling empowered, Dani said out loud with great enthusiasm and certainty, "Tomorrow will be the beginning to an end of bullying. It will be a good day! A good day for all, indeed."

- The End -

CPSIA information can be obtained at www.ICGtesting.com
Printed in the USA
BVOW06s0857070716

454697BV00008B/61/P